THE
tall
BOOK
OF
Mother GOOSE

Mother Goose

THE

tall

BOOK

OF

Mother GOOSE

PICTURED

BY

FEODOR

ROJANKOVSKY

HARPER & ROW, PUBLISHERS
NEW YORK AND EVANSTON

*L*ittle Boy Blue,
        come, blow your horn!
The sheep's in the meadow,
        the cow's in the corn.
Where's the boy who looks
        after the sheep?
He's under the haystack, fast asleep.

Here's Sulky Sue,
What shall we do?
Turn her face to the wall
Till she comes to.

Little Tommy Tittlemouse
Lived in a little house;
He caught fishes
In other men's ditches.

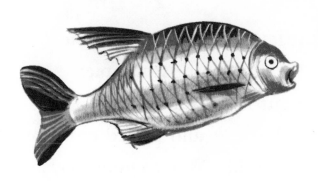

Little Jack Horner sat in the corner,
Eating his Christmas pie;
He put in his thumb,
and pulled out a plum,
And said, "What a good boy am I!"

Little Miss Muffet
Sat on a tuffet,
Eating of curds and whey;
There came a big spider,
And sat down beside her,
And frightened Miss Muffet away.

The Queen of Hearts,
She made some tarts,
All on a summer's day.

The Knave of Hearts,
He stole the tarts,
And took them clean away.

The King of Hearts
Called for the tarts,
And beat the Knave full sore.

The Knave of Hearts
Brought back the tarts,
And vowed he'd steal no more.

There was an old woman
Lived under a hill;
And if she's not gone,
She lives there still.

porridge hot,
porridge cold,
porridge in the pot,
Nine days old.

Some like it hot,
Some like it cold,
Some like it in the pot,
Nine days old.

LITTLE POLLY FLINDERS

Little Polly Flinders
Sat among the cinders,
Warming her pretty little toes!
Her mother came and caught her,
And whipped her little daughter
For spoiling her nice new clothes.

THIS LITTLE PIG

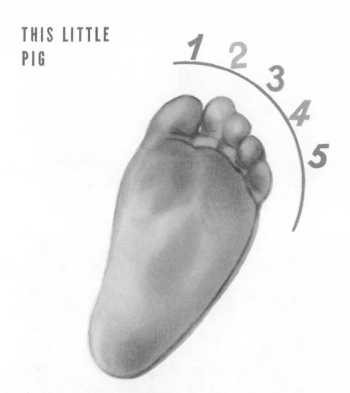

1   This little pig went to market;
2   This little pig stayed home;
3   This little pig had roast beef;
4   This little pig had none;
5   This little pig cried,
      "Wee, wee, wee!"
         All the way home.

There was an old woman
who lived in a shoe.
She had so many children she
didn't know what to do.
She gave them some broth, without any bread,
She whipped them all soundly,
and sent them to bed.

18

There was a piper had a cow
    And he had naught to give her;
He pulled out his pipe and
                played her a tune,
    And bade the cow consider.

The cow considered very well,
   And gave the piper a penny,
And bade him play the other tune,
   "Corn rigs are bonny."

I had a little hobby-horse,
　And it was dapple gray,
Its head was made of pea-straw,
　Its tail was made of hay.
I sold it to an old woman
　For a copper groat;
And I'll not sing my song again
　Without another coat.

Little Betty Blue
　Lost her holiday shoe;
　What shall little Betty do?
　Give her another
　To match the other,
And then she'll walk in two.

As I was going up Pippen Hill,
  Pippen Hill was dirty;
There I met a pretty lass
  And she dropt me a curtsy.
"Little Miss, pretty Miss,
  Blessings light upon you;
If I had half-a-crown a day,
  I'd spend it all upon you."

GOOSEY, GOOSEY
GANDER

Goosey, goosey, gander!
  Where shall I wander?
Upstairs and downstairs
And in my lady's chamber.
There I met an old man
That would not say his prayers.
I took him by the left leg,
And threw him down the stairs.

Three little kittens lost their mittens,
and they began to cry,
"Oh, mother dear, we sadly fear
Our mittens we have lost!"

"What! lost your mittens,
you naughty kittens!
Then you shall have no pie."
"Meow, meow, meow!"

The three little kittens found their
mittens, and they began to cry,
"Oh! mother dear, see here, see here,
Our mittens we have found."

"What! found your mittens,
you good little kittens,
Then you shall have some pie."
"Purr, purr, purr."

The three little kittens put on their
     mittens and soon ate up the pie.
"Oh! mother dear, we greatly fear
   Our mittens we have soiled."

"What! soiled your mittens,
       you naughty kittens!"
Then they began to sigh,
  "Meow, meow, meow!"

The three little kittens washed their
    mittens, and hung them up to dry.
"Oh, mother dear,
          look here, look here,
Our mittens we have washed."

"What! washed your mittens,
         you darling kittens!
But I smell a rat close by!
    Hush! hush! hush!"

SIMPLE SIMON

Simple Simon met a pieman
Going to the fair,
Said Simple Simon to the pieman,
"Let me taste your ware."

Says the pieman to Simple Simon,
  "Show me first your penny."
Says Simple Simon to the pieman,
  "Indeed, I have not any."

He went to catch a dickey bird,
  And thought he could not fail,
Because he'd got a little salt,
  To put upon his tail.

Simple Simon went a-fishing,
  For to catch a whale;
All the water he could find
  Was in his mother's pail.

He went to ride a spotted cow
  That had a little calf,
She threw him down upon the ground,
  Which made the people laugh.

Simple Simon went to look
  If plums grew on a thistle;
He pricked his fingers very much,
  Which made poor Simon whistle.

He went for water in a sieve,
  But soon it all ran through;
And now poor Simple Simon
  Bids you all adieu.

Wee Willie Winkie
  runs through the town,
Upstairs and downstairs,
  in his nightgown;
Rapping at the window,
  crying through the lock,
"Are the children in their beds?
For now it's eight o'clock."

They that wash on Monday
   Have all the week to dry;
They that wash on Tuesday
   Are not so much awry;
They that wash on Wednesday
   Are not so much to blame;
They that wash on Thursday
   Wash for shame;
They that wash on Friday
   Wash in need;
And they that wash on Saturday,
   Oh! they are bad indeed.

Old Mother Hubbard
Went to the cupboard
    To get her poor Dog a bone,
When she came there,
The cupboard was bare,
    And so the poor Dog had none.

She took a clean dish
   To get him some tripe,
But when she came back
   He was smoking a pipe.

She went to the fruiterer's
   To buy him some fruit,
But when she came back
   He was playing the flute.

She went to the tailor's
   To buy him a coat,
But when she came back
   He was riding a goat.

She went to the barber's
   To buy him a wig,
But when she came back
   He was dancing a jig.

She went to the tavern
   For white wine and red,
But when she came back
   The Dog stood on his head.

She went to the cobbler's
   To buy him some shoes,
But when she came back
   He was reading the news.

1, 2,
buckle my shoe;

3, 4,
shut the door;

5, 6,
pick up sticks;

7, 8,
lay them straight;

9, 10,
a good fat hen;

11, 12,
dig and delve;

13, 14,
maids are courting;

15, 16,
maids in the kitchen;

17, 18,
maids are waiting;

19, 20
my platter's empty.

Jack be nimble,
  Jack be quick,
Jack jump over the candlestick.

Hey, diddle, diddle!
The cat and the fiddle,
The cow jumped over the moon;

The little dog laughed
         To see such sport,

And the dish ran away
         with the spoon.

Cross patch,
    Draw the latch,
Sit by the fire and spin;
    Take a cup
    And drink it up,
And call your neighbors in.

Hush-a-bye, baby,
    Daddy is near;
Mamma is a lady,
    And that's very clear.

37

Ride a cockhorse to Banbury Cross,
To see a fine lady upon a white horse.

Rings on her fingers,
and bells on her toes,

She shall have music
wherever she goes.

GREAT A,
LITTLE A

Great A, little a,
Bouncing B!
The cat's in the cupboard,
And can't see me.

There was a little man
and he had a little gun,
And his bullets were made
of lead, lead, lead.

He went to the brook
      and saw a little duck,
And shot it right through
      the head, head, head.

He carried it home
      to his old wife Joan,
And bade her a fire
      to make, make, make,
To roast the little duck
      he had shot in the brook,
And he'd go and fetch
      the drake, drake, drake.

The drake was a-swimming
      with his little curly tail;
The little man made it
      his mark, mark, mark.
He let off his gun,
      but he fired too soon,
And away flew the drake
      with a quack, quack, quack.

What are little boys made of?
   What are little boys made of?
Snakes and snails,
             and puppy-dogs' tails;
And that's what little boys
               are made of.

What are little girls made of?
What are little girls made of?
Sugar and spice and all that's nice;
And that's what little girls
are made of.

TOM, TOM, THE PIPER'S SON

Tom, Tom, the Piper's son,
Stole a pig, and away he run.
The pig was eat, and Tom was beat,
And Tom went crying
                    down the street.

NORTH WIND

The north wind doth blow,
    We soon shall have snow,
And what will poor Robin do then?
    Poor thing!

He'll sit in a barn,
To keep himself warm,
And hide his head under his wing.
    Poor thing!

DOCTOR FOSTER

Doctor Foster went to Gloucester,
In a shower of rain;
He stepped in a puddle
                          up to his middle,
And never went there again.

WINTER

Cold and raw the north winds blow,
Bleak in the morning early;

All the hills are covered with snow;
And winter's now come fairly.

Humpty Dumpty sat on a wall,
Humpty Dumpty had a great fall;

All the King's horses
and all the King's men

Cannot put Humpty Dumpty
together again.

R ain, rain, go away,
   Come again another day;
Little Johnny wants to play.

49

RING A RING
O' ROSES

R ing a ring o' roses,
A pocketful of posies.
Tisha! Tisha!
We all fall down.

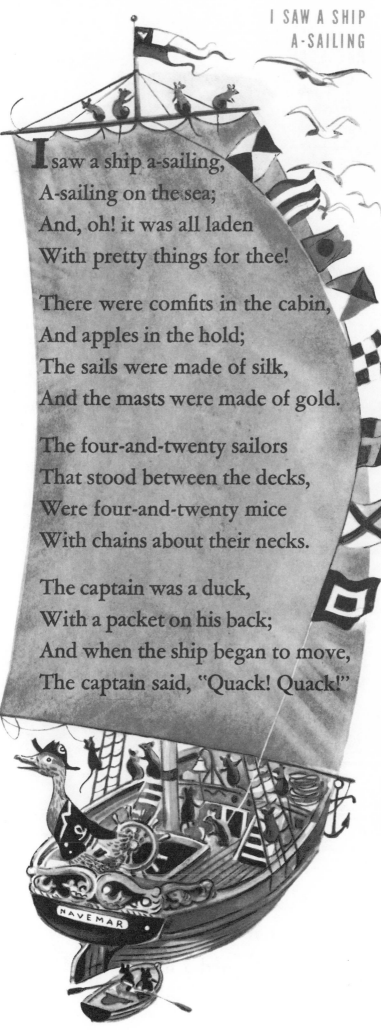

I saw a ship a-sailing,
A-sailing on the sea;
And, oh! it was all laden
With pretty things for thee!

There were comfits in the cabin,
And apples in the hold;
The sails were made of silk,
And the masts were made of gold.

The four-and-twenty sailors
That stood between the decks,
Were four-and-twenty mice
With chains about their necks.

The captain was a duck,
With a packet on his back;
And when the ship began to move,
The captain said, "Quack! Quack!"

"Pussycat, pussycat,
   Where have you been?"
"I've been to London
   To look at the Queen."

"Pussycat, pussycat,
   What did you there?"
"I frightened a little mouse
   Under the chair."

Hickory, Dickory, Dock!
The mouse ran up the clock;
The clock struck one,
And down he run,
Hickory, dickory, dock!

Old King Cole
was a merry old soul,
And a merry old soul was he.
He called for his pipe,
he called for his bowl,
And he called for his fiddlers three.

54

Every fiddler, he had a fine fiddle,
    And a very fine fiddle had he.
Twee, tweedle-dee, tweedle-dee
                went the fiddlers.
    Oh, there's none so rare
                    as can compare
With King Cole and his fiddlers three!

Old King Cole was a merry old soul,
    And a merry old soul was he.
He called for his pipe,
                he called for his bowl,
And he called for his harpers three.

Every harper he had a fine harp,
    And a very fine harp had he.
Twang, twang-a-twang
                went the harpers,
Twee, tweedle-dee, tweedle-dee
                went the fiddlers.
Oh, there's none so rare
                    as can compare
With King Cole
                and his harpers three!

Spring is showery, flowery, bowery;

Summer: hoppy, croppy, poppy;

Autumn: wheezy, sneezy, freezy;

Winter: slippy, drippy, nippy.

Lucy Locket
    lost her pocket,
    Kitty Fisher
    found it;
There was not a penny in it,
    But a ribbon round it.

Little Bo-peep has lost her sheep,
   And can't tell where to find them;
Leave them alone,
          and they'll come home,
Wagging their tails behind them.

Little Bo-peep fell fast asleep,
   And dreamt she heard
          them bleating;
But when she awoke,
        she found it a joke,
For they were still a-fleeting.

Then up she took her little crook,
   Determined for to find them;
She found them indeed,
       but it made her heart bleed,
For they'd left their tails
          behind them.

It happened one day, as Bo-peep did
stray
   Unto a meadow hard by,
There she espied their tails, side by
side,
   All hung on a tree to dry.

She heaved a sigh, and wiped her eye,
   And ran o'er hill and dale,
And tried what she could, as a
shepherdess should,
   To tack each sheep to its tail.

CURLY LOCKS!

Curly-locks! Curly-locks!
           wilt thou be mine?
Thou shalt not wash dishes,
           nor yet feed the swine;
But sit on a cushion,
           and sew a fine seam,
And feed upon strawberries,
           sugar and cream!

Mary had a little lamb,
  Its fleece was white as snow;
And everywhere that Mary went
  The lamb was sure to go.

He followed her to school one day,
  Which was against the rule;
It made the children laugh and play
  To see a lamb at school.

And so the teacher turned him out,
But still he lingered near,
And waited patiently about
Till Mary did appear.

"What makes the lamb love Mary so?"
The eager children cry.
"Oh, Mary loves the lamb, you know,"
The teacher did reply.

To bed, to bed!"
Says Sleepy-head.
"Tarry awhile," says Slow.
"Put on the pan,"
Says greedy Nan.
"We'll sup before we go."

To market,

to market

to buy a fat pig,

Home again,

home again,

jiggety-jig;
To market, to market to buy a fat hog,
Home again, home again,
jiggety-jog.

This is the house that Jack built.
This is the malt
That lay in the house that Jack built.

This is the rat
That ate the malt
That lay in the house
       that Jack built.

This is the cat
That killed the rat
That ate the malt
That lay in the house
    that Jack built.

This is the dog
That worried the cat
That killed the rat
That ate the malt
That lay in the house that Jack built.

This is the cow with the crumpled
    horn,
That tossed the dog
That worried the cat
That killed the rat
That ate the malt
That lay in the house that Jack built.

This is the maiden
      all forlorn,
That milked the cow
            with the
            crumpled horn,
That tossed the dog
That worried the cat
That killed the rat
That ate the malt
That lay in the house that Jack built.

This is the man
      all tattered and torn,
That kissed the
      maiden all forlorn,
That milked the cow
      with the
            crumpled horn,
That tossed the dog
That worried the cat
That killed the rat
That ate the malt
That lay in the house that Jack built.

This is the priest all shaven and shorn,
That married the man all tattered
    and torn,
That kissed the maiden all forlorn,
That milked the cow with the
    crumpled horn,
That tossed the dog
That worried the cat
That killed the rat
That ate the malt
That lay in the house
    that Jack built.

This is the cock
    that crowed in the
        morn,
That waked the priest
    all shaven and shorn,
That married the man all tattered
    and torn,
That kissed the maiden all forlorn,
That milked the cow with the
    crumpled horn,
That tossed the dog
That worried the cat
That killed the rat
That ate the malt
That lay in the house that Jack built.

This is the farmer sowing the corn,
That kept the cock that crowed in
	the morn,
That waked the priest
	all shaven and shorn,
That married the man all tattered
	and torn,
That kissed the maiden all forlorn,
That milked the cow with the
	crumpled horn,
That tossed the dog
That worried the cat
That killed the rat
That ate the malt
That lay in the house that Jack built.

Ride away, ride away,
    Johnny shall ride,
And he shall have pussycat
    Tied to one side;
And he shall have little dog
    Tied to the other,
And Johnny shall ride
    To see his grandmother.

4   5   !

I caught a hare alive;

9   10   !

I let her go again.

JANUARY

January brings the snow,
Makes our feet and fingers glow.

FEBRUARY

February brings the rain,
Thaws the frozen lake again.

MARCH

March brings breezes loud and shrill,
Stirs the dancing daffodil.

APRIL

April brings the primrose sweet,
Scatters daisies at our feet.

MAY

May brings flocks of pretty lambs,
Skipping by their fleecy dams.

JUNE

June brings tulips, lilies, roses,
Fills the children's hands with posies.

JULY

Hot July brings cooling showers,
Apricots and gillyflowers.

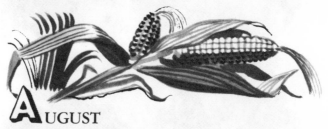

AUGUST

August brings the sheaves of corn,
Then the harvest home is borne.

SEPTEMBER

Warm September brings the fruit,
Sportsmen then begin to shoot

OCTOBER

Fresh October brings the pheasant,
Then to gather nuts is pleasant.

NOVEMBER

Dull November brings the blast,
Then the leaves are whirling fast.

DECEMBER

Chill December brings the sleet,
Blazing fire and Christmas treat.

J. Stout   J. Green

Ding, dong, bell!
Pussy's in the well!
Who put her in?
Little Johnny Green.
Who pulled her out?
Little Johnny Stout.

What a naughty boy was that
To try to drown poor pussy cat
Which never did him any harm,
But killed the mice in his father's
   barn!

pussy

Hickety, pickety, my black hen,
She lays eggs for gentlemen;
Gentlemen come every day
To see what my black hen doth lay.

Punch and Judy
  Fought for a pie;
Punch gave Judy
  A knock in the eye.

Says Punch to Judy,
  "Will you have any more?"
Says Judy to Punch,
  "My eyes are too sore."

Mistress Mary, quite contrary,
How does your garden grow?
With silver bells and cockle shells
And pretty maids all in a row.

Pussy sits by the fire,
    How did she come there?
In walks little doggy,
    Says, "Pussy, are you there?

How do you do, Mistress Pussy?
    Mistress Pussy, how do you. do?"
"I thank you kindly, little dog?
    I do as well as you."

78

COCK:
Lock the dairy door,
Lock the dairy door,

HEN:
Chickle, chackle chee,
I haven't got the key.

"Where are you going,

my pretty maid?"

"I'm going a-milking, sir,"

she said.

"May I go with you,

my pretty maid?"

"You're kindly welcome, sir,"

she said.

"What is your father,

my pretty maid?"

"My father's a farmer, sir," she said.

"What is your fortune,

my pretty maid?"

"My face is my fortune, sir,"

she said.

"Then I can't marry you,
            my pretty maid."
"Nobody asked you, sir," she said.

Handy Pandy, Jack-a-dandy,
    Loves plum cake and sugar candy.
    He bought some at a grocer's shop,
And out he came, hop, hop, hop!

ing a song of sixpence,
       a pocket full of rye;
Four-and-twenty blackbirds
              baked in a pie!
When the pie was opened
           the birds began to sing;
Wasn't that a dainty dish
            to set before the King?

The King was in the countinghouse,
              counting out his money,
The Queen was in the parlor,
           eating bread and honey.
The maid was in the garden,
            hanging out the clothes;
When down came a blackbird
            and snapped off her nose.

ONE MISTY, MOISTY MORNING

One misty, moisty morning,
   When cloudy was the weather,
I chanced to meet an old man
   Clothed all in leather;

He began to compliment,
  And I began to grin—
"How do you do,"
      And "How do you do,"
    And "How do you do" again!

Little Tommy Tucker
  Sings for his supper.
What shall he eat?
  White bread and butter.

How will he cut it
  Without e'er a knife?
How can he marry
  Without e'er a wife?

CRY BABY

Cry, baby, cry,
  Put your finger in your eye,
And tell your mother it wasn't I.

I love little Pussy,
  Her coat is so warm,
And if I don't hurt her,
  She'll do me no harm;
So I'll not pull her tail,
  Nor drive her away,
But Pussy and I
  Very gently will play.

Georgie Porgie, pudding and pie, . . .

When the boys came out to play, ...

. . . Kissed the girls and made them cry.

. . . Georgie Porgie ran away.

Jack and Jill went up the hill
To fetch a pail of water.

Jack fell down and broke his crown,

And Jill came tumbling after.

Then up Jack got and home did trot,
As fast as he could caper.

He went to bed and plastered

his head

With vinegar and brown paper.

Little Robin Redbreast
        sat upon a tree,
Up went Pussycat and
        down went he;
Down came Pussycat
        and away Robin ran;
Says little Robin Redbreast.
        "Catch me if you can!"

Little Robin Redbreast
        jumped upon a wall;
Pussycat jumped after him,
        and almost had a fall.
Little Robin chirped and sang,
        and what did Pussy say?
Pussycat said "Mew"
        and Robin jumped away.

92

THIRTY DAYS
HATH SEPTEMBER

Thirty days hath September,
April, June, and November;
February has twenty-eight alone.
All the rest have thirty-one.
Except in leap year. That's the time
When February's days are

twenty-nine.

Leg over leg,
   As the dog went to Dover;
When he came to a stile,
   Jump, he went over.

Little Nanny Etticoat
   In a white petticoat
   And a red nose;
The longer she stands,
   The shorter she grows.

There was a crooked man,
and he went a crooked mile,

He found a crooked sixpence
against a crooked stile;

He bought a crooked cat,
which caught a crooked mouse,

And they all lived together
in a little crooked house.

🌲 C 🌲 H 🌲 R 🌲 I

Christmas is coming,   . .
Please to put a penny   . .
If you haven't got a penny,   . .
If you haven't got a   . .

S  T   M   A   S

. . the geese are getting fat,
. . in an old man's hat;
. . a ha' penny will do,
. . ha' penny, God bless you.

Once I saw a little bird
  Come hop, hop, hop;
So I cried, "Little bird,
  Will you stop, stop, stop?"

I was going to the window
  To say, "How do you do?"
But he shook his little tail,
  And away he flew.

Ladybird, ladybird,
   fly away home!
Your house is on fire,
      your children all gone;
All but one, and her name is Ann,
   And she crept under
         the pudding pan.

Three blind mice! Three blind mice!
　　See how they run!
　　　　　　See how they run!
They all ran after the farmer's wife,
　　She cut off their tails
　　　　　　with a carving knife.
Did you ever see such a sight
　　　　　　　in your life
　　As three blind mice?

Barber, barber, shave a pig.
How many hairs will make a wig?
Four and twenty; that's enough.
Give the barber a pinch of snuff.

A dillar, a dollar,
A ten-o'clock scholar,
What makes you come so soon?
You used to come at ten o'clock,
And now you come at noon.

Shoe the colt,
    Shoe the colt,
  Shoe the wild mare;
    Here a nail,
    There a nail,
  Yet she goes bare.

103

Pit, pat, well-a-day!
Little Robin flew away.
Where can little Robin be?
Up in yonder cherry tree.

Monday's child
   is fair of face,
Tuesday's child
   is full of grace,

Wednesday's child
   is full of woe,
Thursday's child
   has far to go,
Friday's child is loving and giving,
Saturday's child works hard
   for its living;
But the child that's born
   on the Sabbath day
Is blithe and bonny,
   and good and gay.

105

Where, oh, where
            has my little dog gone?
Oh, where, oh, where can he be?
With his tail cut short,
            and his ears cut long—
Oh, where, oh, where has he gone?

SEESAW, MARGERY DAW

Seesaw, Margery Daw,
    Jackey shall have a new master;
He shall have but a penny a day,
    Because he can't work any faster.

Willy boy, Willy boy,
      where are you going?
I will go with you, if that I may."
"I'm going to the meadow
      to see them a-mowing,
I'm going to help them make the hay."

There was a little girl
    and she had a little curl
Right in the middle of her forehead.
When she was good,
    she was very, very good,

But when she was bad she was horrid.

Polly, put the kettle on,
　　Polly, put the kettle on,
Polly, put the kettle on,
　　And let's have tea.

Sukey, take it off again,
　　Sukey, take it off again,
Sukey, take it off again,
　　They've all gone away.

Here am I, little jumping Joan,
When nobody's with me
I'm always alone.

Needles and pins, needles and pins,
When a man marries
        his trouble begins.

BYE, BABY
BUNTING

Bye, baby bunting,
  Daddy's gone a-hunting,
  To get a little rabbit skin
  To wrap the baby bunting in.

Old Mother Goose, when
She wanted to wander,
Would ride through the air
On a very fine gander.

PETER, PETER, PUMPKIN EATER

Peter, Peter, pumpkin eater,
   Had a wife and couldn't keep her;
He put her in a pumpkin shell,
   And there he kept her very well.

JACK SPRAT

Jack Sprat could eat no fat,
His wife could eat no lean;
And so betwixt them both you see,
They licked the platter clean.

PAT-A-CAKE! PAT-A-CAKE!

Pat-a-cake, pat-a-cake, baker's man!
Bake me a cookie as fast as you can;
Roll it and pat it and mark it with "B"
And put it in the oven for baby and
me.

Taffy was a Welshman,
           Taffy was a thief;
Taffy came to my house
           and stole a piece of beef.

I went to Taffy's house,
           Taffy was not home;
Taffy came to my house
           and stole a marrow-bone.

I went to Taffy's house,
           Taffy was in bed;
I took up the marrow-bone
           and beat him on the head.

Peter Piper picked a peck
            of pickled peppers;
A peck of pickled peppers
            Peter Piper picked.
If Peter Piper picked
            a peck of pickled peppers,
Where's the peck of pickled peppers
            Peter Piper picked?

Rock-a-bye, baby, on the tree top!
When the wind blows
    the cradle will rock,
When the bough breaks
    the cradle will fall;
Down will come baby,
    cradle and all.

Dickory, dickory, dare,
  The pig flew up in the air;
The man in brown soon
  brought him down,
  Dickory, dickory, dare.

The man in the Moon
Came down too soon
To inquire the way
to Norwich;

The man in the South
  he burned his mouth
Eating cold pease porridge.

Bobby Shaftoe's gone to sea,
   Silver buckles on his knee;
He'll come back and marry me,
   Pretty Bobby Shaftoe!

Bobby Shaftoe's fat and fair,
   Combing down his yellow hair;
He's my love forevermore,
   Pretty Bobby Shaftoe.